S0-BBA-906

Most people think of science fiction as a feature of the modern world, but some of the best science fiction stories were written more than a hundred years ago, by the French writer, Jules Verne. Many things that he wrote about have since come true: his stories Twenty Thousand Leagues beneath the Sea, and Around the Moon are now more fact than fiction. Here is one that hasn't come true yet – but who knows, perhaps it will soon!

Published by Ladybird Books Ltd Loughborough Leicestershire UK
Ladybird Books Inc Auburn Maine 04210 USA

Printed in England (3)

A JOURNEY TO THE CENTRE OF THE EARTH

Jules Verne

retold in simple language
by Joyce Faraday

with illustrations by Vivienne Lewis

Ladybird Books

A Journey to the Centre of the Earth

My name is Axel. Some years ago, when
my parents died, I went to live in Hamburg
with my uncle, Professor Lidenbrock, and his
god-daughter Grauben. Unknown to my
uncle, Grauben and I planned to marry one
day. My uncle was a famous scientist who
taught the study of rocks and minerals at the
University. He was a tall, thin, restless man
with a quick temper. I worked as his assistant.
He was fond of me and, as long as I did all
that he wanted, we got on well together.

One day my uncle brought home an old
book about Iceland. As he flicked through
the pages a small piece of paper fell out. On
it were strange Runic signs, and we puzzled
over it for a long time. Suddenly I saw that
by reading the message backwards it made
sense. It read:

'Go to the Sneffels volcano. Each year, on the last day of June, only one of its craters is in shadow. Go down that crater and you will journey to the centre of the Earth. I have done this.'

'That's Arne Saknussemm!' exclaimed my uncle, pointing to the signature. 'He was a great scientist in Iceland in the sixteenth century. The greatest of them all! If he could make such a journey, so can we!'

'We can journey to the centre of the Earth?' I asked in alarm.

'Yes, Axel,' he replied. 'We will follow in his footsteps. And we must leave soon, for we must be at the volcano before July.'

So it was that after a few days, during which we packed tools, instruments and clothes, we left Hamburg. Grauben and I were sad to part but she promised to marry me on my return. I wondered to myself if I *would* return!

It took us about ten days to sail to Reykjavik, the capital of Iceland. My uncle was seasick for the whole voyage, and he only cheered up when we came in sight of the Sneffels volcano. In Reykjavik we stayed at the house of a schoolmaster, who arranged for a guide to take us to the volcano.

The guide's name was Hans. He was tall and strong. He had wise, blue eyes and his chestnut hair reached his broad shoulders. His quiet ways made me feel he could be

trusted. He got on well with my uncle, which was very important.

We planned to start on June 10th. Horses were hired to carry our baggage. We bought tools, rifles, gunpowder and gun-cotton, a first-aid box and strong boots. My uncle packed two compasses, and other instruments which would help us on our journey. I was glad to see he packed two portable electric lamps.

We had food for six months but, to my surprise, our only water was in our water flasks.

'We shall find underground springs and fill our flasks as we need to,' my uncle said when I questioned him.

I hoped he was right. I knew that many of the springs in Iceland are boiling hot. There were other things, too, which worried me about the journey.

'How can we be sure the volcano is extinct?' I asked. 'Just because it hasn't erupted since 1229, we can't be sure it never will again.'

'You need not fear,' the Professor replied. 'There are no signs at all that it will erupt. We'll be quite safe.' I could say no more, since he was not a man to argue with. So we set off.

It took us a week to reach the Sneffels volcano. As we climbed it, the going was hard and the wind bitterly cold. We reached the summit at night and I was worn out. But that night we slept well and in the morning were ready to climb down to the bottom of the crater where we could see three huge holes. It was from these great chimneys that the volcano had last erupted.

My uncle ran from one chimney to the other. It was now the end of June and only one chimney was in shadow. That one was to be our way into the centre of the Earth.

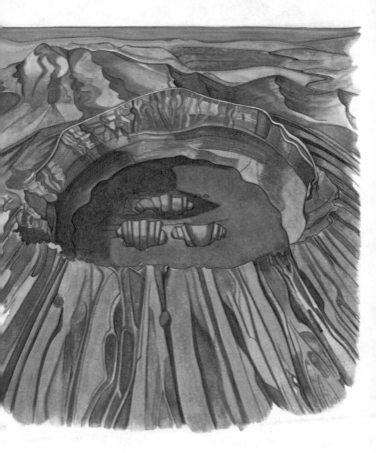

Then my uncle called to me. 'Look!' he cried. He pointed to a block of rock near the chimney, where I could just make out some worn Runic letters carved in the rock.

'Arne Saknussemm,' I read. There could be no doubt that this was the chimney.

On June 30th, with our baggage on our backs, we started on our amazing journey. When I looked down into the chimney, I felt dizzy. The walls went straight down but there were rocks sticking out from the sides. Slowly, with ropes, we let ourselves down from rock to rock.

We rested often and, after ten and a half hours, we reached the bottom of the chimney. Now we were eight hundred and fifty metres down. That night, as I lay down to sleep, I could see a star in the patch of sky above the dark chimney.

The next morning we heaved our packs onto our backs. My uncle lit an electric lamp and we set off through a dark passage. It sloped steeply down and we had difficulty in stopping ourselves from slipping. At long last my uncle called a halt. We ate hungrily and drank some of our water. So far we had seen no underground springs – and already half our water had gone.

The following day I was surprised to find we were walking uphill. It was tiring, and I began to hope we would come up to the surface again. Then I would soon be back in Hamburg with Grauben! But the day after, the gallery took us gently downwards again. We had still not found water and I was worried, for we had only half a flask left.

Still we pressed on. Just as I was wondering how long we could last without water, the light from the lamp showed a solid wall in front of us. We looked for a side passage. There was no way forward. We had to go back to find the right way.

Another day passed, and we drank the last of the water. After two days more we were so weak that we could not go on, and stopped to rest. I begged my uncle to return to the surface. But he was still sure we would find water. I begged Hans to turn back, but he was happy to obey my uncle. 'Trust me, Axel,' my uncle said. There was nothing more I could do. After a sleep we felt stronger and started down another turning. As the day wore on, I became weaker. I began to feel that we were in a prison of rock from which we would never escape. As I fell down in a faint I cried out to my uncle.

When I came round I could dimly see my uncle asleep beside me. A noise made me sit up. Hans was disappearing with the lamp in his hand. Surely our honest guide would not leave us now! I fell into a troubled sleep and was awakened by the return of Hans. He shook my uncle and told him he had heard water running lower in the cave. Quickly we dressed.

Slowly, we went down. The sound of the water gave me new life. But there was no sign of water and, as we went on, the sound grew fainter. We returned to where the sound was loudest. Hans put his ear to the rock wall, where we could hear an underground river running behind the rock. Hans took up his pickaxe and swung blow after blow until the rock gave way. A jet of water shot into the tunnel, and Hans let out a cry of pain as the water hit him. It was boiling hot! When it cooled in our flasks we drank thirstily. The water made a little stream that now flowed along the side of the passage. We called it 'The Hans', after our guide who had saved us.

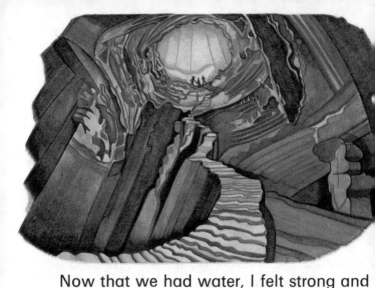

Now that we had water, I felt strong and full of hope again. The stream would alway flow beside us and lead us downwards. Now the passage twisted in all directions. My uncle worked out that we were eleven kilometres under the ground and a hundred and twenty kilometres south-west of Reykjavik. But he wanted to get deeper and was delighted when we came to a steep shaft. It was as steep as the first chimney, but we were able to climb down a huge rock staircase. At the end of that stage of our journey my uncle was better pleased. We were thirty kilometres below the Atlantic Ocean and two hundred kilometres from our starting place.

From then on, each day took us a few kilometres deeper. I led the way, holding my lamp in front of me. Then, suddenly, I found I was alone. I went back and called, but no one answered. Again I shouted. There was no reply. I knew that, with the little stream running beside me, I could easily retrace my steps. I bent down to take a drink. To my horror, there was no water. I had taken a wrong turning!

My way back was hard. There were many side passages and turnings and I could not remember which way I had come.

Turning a corner, I bumped into a solid wall of rock. As I fell I dropped the lamp. It went out and I was alone and lost in the dark. Panic gripped me. I ran from wall to wall, stumbling and shouting. At last I fell down, exhausted.

After a while, I felt my cuts and bruises, then sat in despair, not knowing what to do. In the silence I heard noises like thunder. Then I heard voices. Surely I was going mad! I put my ear to the wall. I still heard voices but could not make out any words. With all my might I shouted, 'Help!' I waited but no answer came. My ear was pressed against the rock. At last I heard my uncle's voice calling me.

'Where are you, Axel?' he called.

'I don't know,' I shouted. 'I'm lost!'

'We'll get you out,' he answered. 'We're
in a big cave with many tunnels leading
into it. If you walk downhill you'll reach it.'

I set off down the steep slope, sliding and
stumbling. Soon the slope became so steep
that I began to fall. The ground disappeared
from under me. I fell down a deep shaft. My
head felt a sharp blow and I remembered
no more.

I slowly opened my eyes. My uncle was kneeling beside me and he cried with joy to see I was alive.

'You are safe, Axel,' he said. 'You will soon be better. Sleep and rest and get strong again.'

I was too weak to ask what had happened to me. I sank into a deep sleep. In the morning my bandaged head ached but I felt stronger. As we ate breakfast, my uncle told me that there had been a rockfall in the tunnel I had been in. I had pitched down with the falling rock, into the cave where now my uncle and Hans were caring for me. It was a miracle that I had not been killed.

Now that I was feeling better, I started to look round the cave. I could see clearly and yet no lamp was burning. There were sounds, too : the sounds of waves and of wind. I thought I must be imagining these things and asked my uncle about them.

'Yes, you are quite right,' he told me.

'Are we back on the surface?' I asked.

'No,' he told me firmly. 'In a while you may see for yourself. When you are fit, we will start on our voyage.'

What could he mean by 'voyage'? I could wait no longer to find out. 'Uncle,' I said, 'I'm strong and well enough now. Show me what you have found.'

We walked out of the dim cave into bright light. My eyes were dazzled by the light shining on water.

'I have called it "The Lidenbrock Sea",' my uncle said proudly. It was indeed a sea. Waves broke on the shore. Cliffs stretched into the distance. The light was not warm like the sun's nor cold like the moon's. It was strong and even. I was sure it was from natural electricity of some kind.

We still seemed to be in a cave. Yet what cave was big enough to hold such a great sea? It was kilometres high, for the clouds

above us were higher than normal clouds. There was no way to judge the length or width of the cave, for the sea stretched further than we could see. After forty days in dark underground tunnels, it was a joy to breathe sea air and to gaze into the distance.

Together, my uncle and I walked along the shore. We came to a vast forest of giant mushroom trees, ten or twelve metres high. There were other plants too, but all of them were plants that had grown on Earth millions of years ago. On the sandy shore we found the dried bones of prehistoric animals. It was like finding treasure.

'Look!' I cried. 'The jawbone of a mammoth.'

My uncle however was eager to explore the sea. The next morning found me perfectly well again. I even went for a swim before eating the breakfast Hans had made for us. Then my uncle worked out that we were fourteen hundred kilometres from Iceland and still moving south-east. This put us about a hundred and thirty kilometres below the mountains of Scotland.

'But how can we get nearer to the centre of the Earth on a flat sea?' I asked him.

'I don't know,' he replied, 'but I'm sure that, if we cross the sea, we'll find more

openings leading downwards.'

I asked him how we could cross the sea without a boat. Hans, he told me, was already at work building a raft.

By evening the raft was finished, and floating on the Lidenbrock Sea.

We loaded the raft the next morning. A blanket served as a sail. With Hans at the tiller, we were ready to leave. Before leaving however we named our little harbour Port Grauben. The thought of Grauben made me long to return home. But the way home was now forward. We sailed out into the sea.

The weather was fine, the clouds high and the wind strong. Hans threw out a fishing line and landed a fine big fish. My uncle said it was a fish long extinct on Earth. Hans

had caught a living fossil! Hours passed and there was no sight of land. My uncle was growing restless. He wanted to get to a lower depth, and began to wonder if we had come the wrong way. In silence we sailed on.

My uncle dropped a pickaxe, tied to a piece of cord, to measure the depth of the sea. The cord was over three hundred and fifty metres long, but it did not touch bottom. Then, when we pulled the pickaxe back on board, we found teeth marks on the iron. Nothing less than a monster crocodile could have made such marks! I checked our guns in case we should need them. We could feel danger everywhere, but saw nothing. Weary of watching, I fell asleep. A violent shock awoke me. The raft was lifted up and thrown thirty metres or more.

Hans pointed to a dark mass rising and falling in the water a short distance away. It looked like a giant porpoise.

My uncle pointed to a huge sea-lizard and a crocodile with rows of teeth.

'And there's a monster whale,' he yelled. 'See it lashing the water with its tail!'

We all stared at the sight in amazement and horror. The smallest of these animals could snap our raft in half. More terrifying animals appeared – a huge turtle and a serpent ten metres long, darting its head above the waves. All the monsters were moving towards us and I held my rifle at the ready. The serpent and the crocodile circled nearer. The rest seemed to disappear. I was about to shoot when Hans stopped me.

The monsters were not going to attack us. Instead they flew at one another, lashing the water and rising out of the foaming waves. We then saw that there were only two animals. One had the snout of a porpoise, the head of a lizard and the teeth of a crocodile. We were seeing a prehistoric ichthyosaurus fighting a plesiosaurus!

The ichthyosaurus must have been thirty metres long. Its great jaws were terrifying. The body of the plesiosaurus was protected by a thick shell and its long neck rose ten metres above the waves. The great beasts fought with fury, using teeth and tails. Huge waves nearly overturned us. For over two hours they fought. Then both animals sank below the surface. The head of the wounded plesiosaurus rose up, whipping and waving, coiling and uncoiling. Slowly it lost its strength and lay still. The battle was over. We breathed again but feared the ichthyosaurus still below the sea. For the moment we were safe.

About midday on the sixth day on the raft we heard a roaring noise. At first I thought it was waves breaking on rocks, or a waterfall. Hans climbed the mast and saw a great jet of water rising from the sea. We thought it was another giant sea-monster! By eight o'clock that evening we could make out something about a kilometre long lying in the sea. The jet of water rained down upon it. I was terrified.

'It's an island,' Hans suddenly called out.

'But what about the jet of water?' I asked.

'A geyser,' my uncle answered. 'It's like those in Iceland.'

Now the jet of water looked beautiful. The light sparkled on the water and made a rainbow. We landed on the island and the ground trembled under our feet. It was burning hot. The water from the geyser was boiling and filled the air with clouds of steam. Such heat must have come from fires burning deep underground. I was sure that if we went deeper we must reach the burning depths. But my uncle became angry when I told him of my fears. I kept quiet, for now I could be sure of nothing.

29

Before leaving the island I noted that we were one thousand and eighty kilometres from Port Grauben where we had set sail on this sea. We must have been somewhere

under England. The following day the wind was strong and we sailed even faster. The clouds thickened and the sky grew darker. The air was full of electricity as if gathering for a storm. The coming storm added to my uncle's anger. He did not want it to hold us up. Then the wind dropped, and nothing moved.

I asked if I should take down the sail and mast before the storm started, but my uncle said 'no' to this.

'Let the wind carry us away!' he said. 'Perhaps we shall then reach the other side of this endless sea!'

As if in answer, the wind rose and became a hurricane. The raft tossed and bounded ahead. We clung to it as the wind raged. Hans however sat calmly at the tiller. The electricity in the air played on his hair. He seemed to have a strange light round his head. The wind blew us along at a great speed. The rain beat down. Thunder rolled and lightning flashed all round us. Massive hailstones fell. They made a bright electric flash as they hit our tools or any metal. Even the crests of the waves were edged with flames.

It seemed as if the whole world was blowing up in a great explosion. For three days we were blown before the gale. I clung to the mast and feared we would drown. Then a ball of fire landed on the raft. The mast and sail were flung into the air. The fireball was half white and half blue and about twenty five centimetres across. It jumped from rope to deck and from our sacks to boxes, spinning fast as it moved. For a second it touched a bag of gunpowder. By a miracle we were not blown up.

The fireball rolled near my foot and I tried to move away. But my foot was held fast to

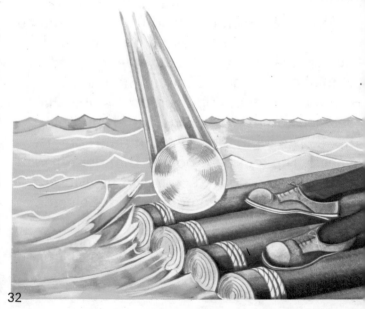

the deck. I saw that all the iron of the raft was magnetised by the fireball. The iron nails in my boots were clinging to an iron plate in the deck! With a pull I freed myself. The fireball burst in a blaze. Flames covered us. Then all went dark. We threw ourselves to the deck to rest and regain our strength. The wind still raged but we were too tired to care. I only knew that we were being carried along at a great speed and must have passed under France.

Dazed and weak we were at last flung up on a rocky coast. I would have been dashed to pieces had not Hans pulled me out of the wild sea. He saved my uncle too, and then went back to save what he could of our goods from the wreck.

We awoke to a beautiful day and felt rested. My uncle was even bright and cheerful now that we had crossed the sea. 'Now we can really start going down again,' he said. My heart sank at the thought of going yet deeper into the Earth. I longed to get back to Hamburg and to Grauben.

Hans had collected together our goods from the wreck. Our guns had gone, but the gunpowder and gun-cotton were safe and dry. We still had a compass, some other instruments and tools and ropes. Most of our food had been saved and we had enough for four months. After breakfast we sat down to work out where we were and to plan our next step.

'Hans is mending the raft,' my uncle said, 'but I don't think we'll need it again. I've an idea we'll not get out the way we came in.'

I wondered what he meant and how he knew.

As the storm had blown us to the south-east, we agreed we must be somewhere under the Mediterranean. We looked at the compass to check our position, but what we saw puzzled us. We checked again. According to the compass we were back on the side of the sea from which we had started. Sadly, we decided that the wind had changed during the storm and driven us back.

My uncle was at first surprised and then angry. He stormed and raged. I begged him to turn back but nothing would make him change his mind. Hans quietly obeyed his master. Again there was nothing I could do but go on.

Whilst Hans worked on the raft, my uncle and I set out to explore. We walked along the shore, which was covered with the shells of prehistoric animals. We also found some huge turtle shells. Soon we came upon piles of bones. There were the bones of every kind of animal that had ever lived.

'Look at this, Axel!' the Professor called in a trembling voice. 'A human skull!'

I was no less amazed than my uncle.

A few more steps brought an even greater shock. There, in the dust, was the body of a prehistoric man. It still had flesh, hair and nails and seemed almost alive! We had seen the bones of dinosaurs and also seen live ones. Here was the body of a prehistoric man. Would we find a live man?

We walked on. In about a kilometre we came to a great forest. There were trees and plants from a world of millions of years ago. But these plants were not green. Without sunlight they were all a faded brown. My uncle pushed on through the bushes and into the forest. Under the trees something moved. We stopped and peered through the leaves. There, before us, was a herd of prehistoric elephants, the gigantic mastodons. They were feeding on leaves which they tore from the trees with their trunks.

'Come on,' whispered my uncle. 'Let's go on.'

'It wouldn't be safe if they charged,' I warned him.

'Perhaps not,' he agreed in a low voice. 'Look over there!'

I could not believe my eyes. Leaning against a tree was a man. He was keeping watch over his herd of mastodons. He was at least four metres tall, and taller than the mastodons. His head was as big as a bison's and he had a thick mane of matted hair. He held the branch of a tree in his hand.

This was no place to stay and we got away quickly. Once out of the forest, we ran towards the shore. We then looked for signs that we were near Port Grauben but could find none. As we walked on the beach I saw something shining in the sand I picked up a rusty dagger. We looked at it carefully. The dagger was old, and rust showed it had lain in the sand for a long time.

'This belonged to someone who came here before us!' said my uncle. 'Perhaps we'll find something to show us the way to the centre of the Earth.'

We searched the cliffs and at last found a dark tunnel. By the entrance, scratched into the rock, were Runic signs.

'A.S.! Arne Saknussemm!' shouted my uncle.

Once more we knew we were on the right path.

'I can't explain how we travelled north,' my uncle said. 'I was sure we were going south-east. But here we are, in the right place. That's all that matters!'

We went back to Hans. Together we sailed the raft along the coast until we reached Arne Saknussemm's tunnel. We went ashore. I was keen to explore the passage, and when my uncle lit his electric lamp, I led the way.

The opening led straight into the tunnel, but in a short distance we found our way blocked by a huge rock.

'How did Saknussemm get through?' I asked angrily.

'This rock must have fallen since he was here,' my uncle replied.

'Then let's use our gun-cotton and blow it out of our way,' I suggested.

Hans got his pickaxe and made a hole in the rock. He packed it with gun-cotton. Then my uncle and I made a fuse, using damp gunpowder in a linen tube. By midnight all was ready.

We were awake and ready early the next morning. We decided that I would light the fuse and then join the others on the raft. While the fuse burned we would push out with the raft so that when the explosion came, we would be away from danger.

I picked up the fuse and opened my lantern to get a light. Then I lit the fuse and made sure it was burning well. I raced back to the raft. Hans pushed off. At a safe distance from shore we waited. The second ticked by. Suddenly, the rock exploded. We stared into a bottomless pit. The sea swelled into a great wave and the raft tossed madly. We were thrown to the deck and there was no light. In the darkness the roar of water filled my ears. We had blown up a rock which blocked the entrance to a pit leading down to the centre of the Earth. Now that the rock had gone, the sea could rush in, carrying us with it!

We were rushing on roaring water down
into the Earth. We clung to one another, and
to the raft. We rushed down and down at
high speed in complete darkness. Then
Hans managed to light a lantern, and we
saw that all our cargo had gone except for
a compass and a little food. The water fell
steeply and sometimes we spun round.
When the lantern burned out I shut my eyes

and waited. Our speed increased. The fall grew steeper. Time seemed endless. There was a sudden shock, and the raft almost stopped.

We had hit a water-spout and the water was falling on the raft. I was sure we would be drowned. But we surfaced and all was silence. After the roaring of the water it seemed strangely quiet.

'We're going up!' called my uncle.

Hans lit a torch. We were rising on the water in a narrow shaft. Escape seemed impossible. As the water rose, the heat grew greater. Soon the water below us was boiling. The walls of the shaft were burning hot. In the light of the torch I thought I saw the rocks move. There was a loud explosion. The walls of the shaft shook. In terror, I looked at my uncle. To my surprise he was calm.

'The Earth is moving!' I called to him.

'This is no earthquake, Axel,' he said. 'We're in the chimney of an erupting volcano! This is the best thing that could have happened to us! We will be carried up to the surface!'

All we could do was sit and wait whilst we were carried upwards.

Below the water were burning rocks. If w[e] ever reached the surface the rocks would b[e] hurled out in a red-hot explosion.

Towards morning the air grew hotter and
our speed increased. I saw tunnels into the
walls of the shaft. Smoke and flames
poured from them. Our raft floated on red-
hot lava. The heat was terrible. The raft
whirled round in a shower of hot ash.
Flames sprang up all around us. It seemed
all must be lost. I fainted.

When I came to my senses I felt Hans' strong hand on me. We were lying on the side of a volcano. We were all cut and bruised, but not badly hurt. I could not believe that we were lying in the sun on the surface of the Earth.

'Where can we be?' I asked.

'Perhaps the compass can help us,' said my uncle.

I checked the compass. 'If the compass is right,' I told him, 'we're at the North Pole!'

We looked at the countryside around us. Below we saw trees. There were olives, figs and vines. The sun was hot. This was not Iceland! We decided to go down the slope of the volcano and look for a village.

We were tired and dirty and our clothes were in rags. We found a stream and gladly cooled ourselves and drank thirstily.

A small boy saw us and started to run away but Hans caught him. My uncle spoke to the boy in German and French but he did not answer. Then, in answer to a question in Italian, the boy replied, 'Stromboli.' We were on Stromboli in the Mediterranean Sea. We had travelled from the volcano in Iceland to Stromboli in the Mediterranean. What a journey we had made through the Earth!

We went down to the coast where the people thought we had been shipwrecked. They gave us food and clothes and, in two days, sent us on our way home. As we sat quietly in boats and trains we puzzled over the mystery of the compass. But all this was forgotten when we reached Hamburg.

Grauben was overjoyed to see us. The news of our strange journey had spread through the country. Soon it spread through the world. Great scientists came to talk with the famous Professor Lidenbrock and his assistant. The quiet Hans soon felt homesick, and we sadly watched him leave to return to Iceland. So, at last, everyone was happy. All had turned out well for us. But there was still the mystery of the compass.

One day, in the study, I picked up the compass and looked at it. The answer was clear.

'Look, uncle,' I said. 'The needle points south instead of north. That fireball in the storm magnetised all the iron. It changed the poles of the compass. It made it point south, not north!'

'Of course,' said the Professor. 'So simple that I never thought of it.'

With that last mystery solved my uncle became a very contented man. I could not have been happier. As we had planned, Grauben and I were married and we all three lived happily together in Hamburg.

Stories . . . that have stood the test of time

Ladybird titles cover a wide range of subjects and reading ages.
Write for a free illustrated list from the publishers:
LADYBIRD BOOKS LTD Loughborough Leicestershire England
and USA – LADYBIRD BOOKS INC Auburn, Maine 04210